Spay

by Madison Fiedler

FOR PRODUCTION INQUIRIES

UNITED STATES AND CANADA
info@concordtheatricals.com
1-866-979-0447

UNITED KINGDOM AND EUROPE
licensing@concordtheatricals.co.uk
020-7054-7298

Each title is subject to availability from Concord Theatricals Corp., depending upon country of performance. Please be aware that *SPAY* may not be licensed by Concord Theatricals Corp. in your territory. Professional and amateur producers should contact the nearest Concord Theatricals Corp. office or licensing partner to verify availability.

No one shall make any changes in this title(s) for the purpose of production. No part of this book may be reproduced, stored in a retrieval system, scanned, uploaded, or transmitted in any form, by any means, now known or yet to be invented, including mechanical, electronic, digital, photocopying, recording, videotaping, or otherwise, without the prior written permission of the publisher. No one shall share this title(s), or any part of this title(s), through any social media or file hosting websites.

For all inquiries regarding motion picture, television, online/digital and other media rights, please contact Concord Theatricals Corp.

MUSIC AND THIRD-PARTY MATERIALS USE NOTE

Licensees are solely responsible for obtaining formal written permission from copyright owners to use copyrighted music and/or other copyrighted third-party materials (e.g. artworks, logos) in the performance of this play and are strongly cautioned to do so. If no such permission is obtained by the licensee, then the licensee must use only original music and materials that the licensee owns and controls. Licensees are solely responsible and liable for clearances of all third-party copyrighted materials, including without limitation music, and shall indemnify the copyright owners of the play(s) and their licensing agent, Concord Theatricals Corp., against any costs, expenses, losses and liabilities arising from the use of such copyrighted third-party materials by licensees. For music, please contact the appropriate music licensing authority in your territory for the rights to any incidental music.

IMPORTANT BILLING AND CREDIT REQUIREMENTS

If you have obtained performance rights to this title, please refer to your licensing agreement for important billing and credit requirements.

The world premiere of *SPAY* opened at Rivendell Theatre Ensemble (Artistic Director, Tara Mallen) on March 17, 2022. It was directed by Georgette Verdin, with scenic design by Lindsay Mummert, sound design by Joyce Ciesil, costume design by Becca Duff, lighting design by Michael Mahlum, props design by Rowan Doe, dramaturgy by Catherine Yu, community engagement programming by Denise Yvette Serna and Brit Cooper Robinson, and original compositions by Jane Baxter Miller. The stage manager was Deya Friedman and the assistant director was Rashada Dawan. The cast was as follows:

NOAH . . . . Rae Gray

HARPER. . . . . Krystel McNeil

AUBREY. . . . . Tara Mallen

JACKSON. . . . . .Spencer Huffman

The understudies/extension cast included:

NOAH . . . . .Jill Oliver

HARPER. . . . . Maya Jahan Abram

AUBREY. . . . . Mary Cross

JACKSON. . . . . Anthony Baldasare

SPAY was also developed through readings at BoHo Theatre, Florida Repertory Theatre, TheatreLab at Florida Atlantic University, Rivendell Theatre Ensemble, and at Actor's Express as part of the 2019 National Showcase of New Plays. It appeared on the 2020 Kilroys List, which honored plays whose scheduled premieres had been delayed or canceled due to the pandemic.

In 2023, *SPAY* was awarded the American Theatre Critics Association's (ATCA) M. Elizabeth Osborn Award, which recognizes the work of a playwright who has not yet received a major production, such as a Broadway or Off-Broadway engagement.

CHARACTERS

NOAH – Harper's half-sister, twenty. White. An active user.

Swings between goofy sweetness and rage. Anxious, childlike. Fervently attached to people.

HARPER – Noah's half-sister, twenty-five. Biracial/Black. Not a user. A kindergarten teacher.

Patient, tough-love, deeply hopeful. Has been the adult in this family since early adolescence.

AUBREY – Project Protection representative, late forties to mid-fifties. White. Not from around here.

Watchful, bright, ceaselessly polite. A Midwestern sensibility.

JACKSON – Noah's long-time on-again off-again boyfriend and dealer, twenty-one. Not a user. White or assimilated into whiteness in this town.

Affable, playful, more vulnerable than he lets on.

SETTING

Williamson, Mingo County, West Virginia, USA. A town just shy of three thousand people. Small enough for the neighbors to know what's what, too spread out for small-town charm. Auto shops, Baptist churches. "Heart of the Billion-Dollar Coalfield." "Pilliamson."

The interior of Harper's house, once her and Noah's childhood home. An aging, confined space with crayon drawings on the fridge and toys around the floor, soft ones. A kitchen, a living room with an oversized couch, one door to the outside and one to Benny's room. Off: a small dining area, Harper's bedroom, the bathroom.

TIME

The present, mid-September.

AUTHOR'S NOTES

Noah, Harper, and Jackson have West Virginian accents to varying degrees (Harper masks it somewhat to speak more "properly"; Noah and Jackson don't try to).

A slash (/) indicates an overlap in dialogue.

Words in parentheses ( ) are spoken under the breath or as an aside.

In addition to everyone involved in productions,
special thanks to Hallie Gordon, Lucy Powis,
Ann & Robert H. Lurie Children's Hospital for providing
Narcan training for artists + audiences;
all of Rivendell's town hall panelists on harm reduction
and community action;
my family and friends, who are the world & more to me;
Chase, forever, in every life.

Scene One

*(**HARPER** enters the house, irritated and silent. **NOAH** trails in her wake. She's in the early stages of withdrawal: cold sweats and shaking. Neither has slept. **HARPER** takes off her shoes and looks pointedly to **NOAH** to do the same. She does. **HARPER** puts her purse on the counter, locks the door behind her, glances out the window and closes the blinds. Pours herself a glass of water and drinks the whole thing. Turns on the radio, to blaring static, changes the channel but it's all static. Hits the thing and it goes silent. She glances over at **NOAH**, who's been hovering behind her.)*

HARPER. Are you thirsty? / You're probably dehydrated.

NOAH. Naw, nope. Just achey, I'm / fine.

HARPER. I read that you'd get dehydrated.

NOAH. I don't feel thirsty.

HARPER. Dehydrated and thirsty are / different.

NOAH. Don't feel dehydrated neither.

HARPER. Either.

NOAH. What?

HARPER. Not neither.

NOAH. Oh my Lord Harper.

HARPER. Just, siddown and I'll tend to you in a / minute.

NOAH. Don't need tending to.

HARPER. Ohhhkay.

> (**NOAH** *sits on the couch, plays with her sleeves. In the kitchen,* **HARPER** *begins a well-established routine: she opens the silverware drawer, takes out all the spoons, dumps them in a plastic bag, tucks it in her purse. Next, opens the top shelf and pulls out a piggybank, adds it to her purse too. Takes twine out of another drawer, rubber bands, matches. She pours a glass of water and carries it over to* **NOAH**, *whose hands shake. Some water spills. She glances at* **HARPER**, *places the water on the table. Immediately:)*

Are you cold?

NOAH. Did you *read* I'd get cold?

HARPER. You're shaking, I can see you shaking, you were shaking / the whole way home.

NOAH. Yeah well it's not cause I'm cold it's like a million degrees in here.

HARPER. Didn't know, which is why I asked.

NOAH. Which is why I'm sayin' no.

HARPER. Great.

NOAH. Yeah, great.

HARPER. This is really how you're gonna act right now?

NOAH. I'm probably just dehydrated.

> *(Pause.)*

HARPER. Really, Noah? This is how you treat me after these past eighteen hours? After I spend the night at / Memorial, *awake* the whole time by the way, to make sure you're still alive?

NOAH. Okay okay okay I'm sorry but everything hurts, I feel like crap, I didn't ask you for any of –

HARPER. You're the one who wanted to come to my home, wanted to have a talk.

NOAH. I did, I do, my mind's just everywhere and I need a minute –

HARPER. Well, take your minute on the couch and drink some water. We're talking here, I'm not hauling you over to Jackson's.

NOAH. He can come by later, pick me up.

HARPER. Wasn't he gonna "come by" the hospital at some point?

NOAH. He got busy.

HARPER. Busy, oh.

> (**HARPER** *gives the water to* **NOAH.** *She begrudgingly drinks.*)

NOAH. I know. That you're mad.

HARPER. Good start.

NOAH. Quit talking to me like I'm some kinda lowlife–

HARPER. You're gonna get people in this town calling you a lowlife, people who know a whole lot of lowlives personally, people who've been lowlives themselves but still somehow managed to not overdose in / front of a bunch of *children* at a *kindergarten baseball game.*

NOAH. I know. I know. I know I know I know I'm *sorry.*

HARPER. Oh you're sorry? Oh good. Oh that helps.

NOAH. Can we just start this over, we don't have to talk about the game right / away.

HARPER. No, we're gonna talk about the game.

NOAH. I know I fucked up.

HARPER. Do not curse in my home, a child lives here.

NOAH. Benny's not *home*. Wait where's Benny?

HARPER. Now you ask where's Benny.

He's at the McManns', they offered to take him after. Slept without his special blanket, so he'll be a mess today.

NOAH. I'm sorry he had to do that.

HARPER. Wouldn't be safe to have him here, so.

NOAH. Benny will always be safe around me.

(**HARPER** *laughs, without humor to it.*)

Don't laugh I'm serious.

HARPER. A *public park* with a *bunch of six-year-olds* playing / a *game of* –

NOAH. I wasn't *planning to.*

HARPER. Well. Spontaneous or otherwise, what you do affects people, Noah, here I am waiting to see if you live through the night and I've got voicemails from Principal Ryan saying we need to talk and there's a headline about you on the Daily's website and none of that even matters compared to the fact that: because of you, a whole team of children is traumatized.

These kids are *surviving,* this is a survival town is where we're at, Noah. I got three kids whose parents died this *year.* I've got kids who come in hungry and kids who wear the same clothes each day, but the school can give them this one small thing, this game, this afternoon where they're safe and they're happy and they've got grown-ups paying attention to them, cheering them on. And then –

NOAH. I know.

HARPER. You almost *died.* You looked *dead,* those kids thought they watched you / *die.*

NOAH. I was never gonna–

HARPER. I'm sure you've never actually watched an overdose, Noah, but it's not a pretty sight, all twitching and slumped over the bleachers with your eyes rolled back in your head –

NOAH. Stop.

HARPER. The looks people gave me, like I was *contaminated*, somehow –

NOAH. Look, sorry if I embarrassed you, is that what you / want me to –?

HARPER. Embarrassed is the last thing on my mind. Had to call an ambulance, I don't even *know* what that bill's gonna look like but what I *do* know's a kindergarten teacher salary won't be payin' it off anytime soon, that's for dang / sure –

NOAH. I was fine by the time they got there!

HARPER. You *used in front of Benny.*

My, our Benny.

(Beat.)

NOAH. I didn't. Think he'd be there.

HARPER. He wants to join the school team when he gets to kindergarten, I bring him to all the games, don't you ask him about anything?

NOAH. Oh do not start with me on Benny you give me a Sunday a *month.*

HARPER. I give you more than you have proven you can handle.

NOAH. I am his *I am his mother.*

HARPER. We're not playing that game.

NOAH. You act like he ain't mine, like –

HARPER. I act as his *guardian*, you made me his guardian.

I have to make hard decisions for his own good, and I've been lenient this far, but I can't keep living on promises you don't keep.

NOAH. What're you even –

HARPER. I thought about it in the ambulance and the hospital and the whole way back and I can't have you around Benny anymore, I will not be our mother and I will not raise a child around a junkie.

NOAH. Okay okay Jesus, I get it, it won't happen again.

HARPER. I'm serious. I'm cutting you off.

NOAH. You can't do that. Wait you can't *do* that.

HARPER. I can and I think Child Protective Services can legally enforce that. Kinship adoptions can become closed adoptions real quick, and they do, / all the time.

NOAH. But it was just *it was one time* I've followed your rules I've been clean every time I seen him for the last / year –

HARPER. He's not a baby anymore, he remembers everything he sees here on out.

NOAH. I *know how old he is*.

HARPER. He asked if Auntie Noah was sick again. He asked if he could give you his special blanket to help you get / better.

NOAH. I'm an hour out of the hospital I still got the stupid bracelet on and you're gonna tell me you're takin' my kid away from me?

HARPER. *(Looking down.)* Noah.

NOAH. You don't *get* it look at me in the face I am telling you I'm gonna get clean for real it'll be *different* this time. I've been *good* with Sunday dinners I ain't missed one since last year, I've done everything you told me to and –

Look at me, Harps.

> (**HARPER** *looks at* **NOAH**.)

If I don't get to see him grow I don't know what I'll do with myself.

Please. I mean it this time, I'll change, I'll be better, I'll do anything.

> (*Beat.*)

HARPER. Prove it.

NOAH. Prove it?

HARPER. You mean it this time, give me action items, make a list. Now.

NOAH. Does that mean you'll let me –

HARPER. List, now.

NOAH. I'll up my hours at Waffle House. I'll send you my schedule so you always know where I am.

HARPER. Good, fine. What else?

NOAH. I'll I'll look into methadone clinics.

HARPER. Would Williamson Comp take you / back?

NOAH. There's a new one in Chattaroy if they won't.

HARPER. I'll look into it, what else?

NOAH. I'll ask around about Suboxone.

HARPER. You'll see *Dr. Kierney* about Suboxone, nothing illegal.

NOAH. Haven't seen Dr. Kierney since I was sixteen.

HARPER. You'll see him now.

NOAH. Yeah sure okay.

> (*Half a beat:* **HARPER** *makes a decision.*)

HARPER. You'll move back in with me and Benny, at least for a while. You'll stay here, on the couch, there'll be rules but you'll stay here so I can take care of you. You're gonna let me take care of you.

NOAH. I can play with Benny?

HARPER. With my supervision. What else?

NOAH. I don't – I can't think of.

HARPER. If you're going to keep the relationship you've got with Benny, I need more from you. I need it to be harder for you to make a mistake, to even have the option to / use –

NOAH. I could break up with Jackson.

(Pause.)

I mean. If I'm already staying here for a while.

HARPER. Yeah?

NOAH. Son of a bitch didn't even show up at the hospital. Had tubes in my nose to breathe and shit and he didn't even show.

HARPER. The cursing's gotta stop.

NOAH. Sorry.

HARPER. You'll break up with Jackson.

NOAH. Says he loves me and didn't even show.

HARPER. You'll break up with Jackson?

NOAH. Yeah. Yes.

HARPER. You won't buy from Jackson?

NOAH. Wouldn't be able to get it for free anymore, so.

HARPER. Is that supposed to be a joke?

NOAH. I can still be funny.

I can still – I'm me, okay?

(She gets lightheaded, sits down, squints her eyes shut.)

HARPER. You're alright.

NOAH. I know it's bad. I know I messed up.

HARPER. I know you know.

NOAH. I was clean for nine months, remember? I did it, I could do it again.

HARPER. I know you could. It's why I push you hard.

NOAH. You called me a junkie. You think I'm a junkie?

HARPER. No. I think you have a disease.

NOAH. Don't know if I'd rather be a junkie or diseased.

*(Pause. **NOAH** chews her fingernails.)*

HARPER. Drink your water.

Scene Two

(Two days later. The space feels a little smaller: the couch has been made up like a bed, and a couple oversized bags of Noah's things are tucked around it.)

*(**NOAH** is alone in the kitchen making coffee, hair wet, in a too-big bathrobe. Her withdrawal symptoms have worsened: she's nauseous, sweaty, shivery. As soon as the coffee is done brewing, she takes a massive sip, burning her tongue. She yelps.)*

NOAH. God-damned motherfucker son of a bitch.

(She runs cold water over her tongue in the sink. She finds some sugar, looks for a spoon to no avail. Opens some more drawers, notices what's been removed. Uh-huh. She dumps a bunch of sugar in, stirs it with a fork.)

(A dog barks outside and she jumps. She opens all the blinds, cracks the windows – a breeze comes into the kitchen and she feels it, enjoys it. She turns on the radio to blaring static, fiddles with it clumsily, presses a couple buttons. A bluegrass-country song, something wistful, comes through the static. A little proud of herself, she goes to sip the coffee again when there's a knock at the door.)*

(She jumps, spilling half the coffee down her front. Another knock. She sets down the coffee on the counter and moves to go change.)

---

* A license to produce *Spay* does not include a performance license for any third-party or copyrighted music. Licensees should create an original composition or use music in the public domain. For further information, please see the Music and Third-Party Materials Use Note on page iii.

JACKSON. *(Offstage.)* Noah?

> *(She stops in her tracks.)*

Baby?

> *(**NOAH** exhales. She crouches, silently screams into her hands.)*
>
> *(More knocks. Then, hammering.)*

Noah, baby, it's me!

It's me, Jackson!

Noah?

> *(**NOAH** stands far from the door.)*

I don't wanna fight I just wanna talk!

> *(**NOAH** finger-combs her hair, chews her fingers.)*

Baby, I know you're stayin' here. So quit waitin' for me to leave cause I won't! I'll sleep on the welcome mat!

> *(**NOAH** slumps against the wall.)*

I got you a present!

> *(**NOAH** looks up.)*

You want a present, baby?

Just come to the door.

> *(**NOAH** stands up slowly.)*

Lemme give my baby a present at least. Lemme show you how much I love you.

> *(**NOAH** crosses the room, stands pressed against the door. She hits it hard. A muffled "Ow" from the other side.)*

NOAH. You think I'm stupid?

I don't want your god-damn present, Jackson.

JACKSON. *(Offstage.)* I can tell you're mad at me but I don't know why!

NOAH. Rack your brain, Jackson.

JACKSON. *(Offstage.)* Open the door so you can explain it to me!

NOAH. I don't *want* to. Just / go.

JACKSON. *(Offstage.)* Lemme see that beautiful face. I've missed that face, Noah, I gotta see it. *Please.*

Lemme see my little honeybee's face.

> *(Short pause.)*

NOAH. It don't look good.

JACKSON. *(Offstage.)* Well that just ain't possible, it's my favorite face in the world.

> *(**NOAH** unlocks the door. Pause. She opens it a crack. **JACKSON** stands at the doorway holding a bunch of flowers pulled up from the garden, roots still attached.)*

Hi, baby.

NOAH. You saw my face, now you can go.

> *(**JACKSON** wrenches the door open and walks inside.)*

JACKSON. Did you think you could just up and leave me without talking about it? You disappear for two days and I don't knock on no doors asking questions?

NOAH. You disappeared at the game.

JACKSON. You know how much product I had on me, baby, law comes I gotta go.

NOAH. I was damn near *dead.*

JACKSON. You wasn't gonna – Harper was there, no way you die under Harper's watch.

NOAH. You knew Harper was there?

JACKSON. – It ain't that big of a park. We waved.

NOAH. I don't remember.

JACKSON. You were floating ten feet high, time we got there.

NOAH. And you let me do more?!

JACKSON. I don't let you do nothing, you pay for the product and you're a grown-ass adult can do / what she wants!

NOAH. I'm a grown-ass adult dating your childish self and you *let me OD.*

JACKSON. You think I'm a scientist or something? Shoot, baby, I didn't know you'd tweak out like that.

NOAH. Gee, Jackson, you know how to say just what a girl wants to hear.

> (**JACKSON** *takes a step forward. He speaks more gently.*)

JACKSON. Baby, I'm all tripped-up nerves and Red Bull brain right now, I can't help sayin' the wrong things. I shouldn't've left the game, that's why you're mad. I get it now.

NOAH. You up and left, I up and left, we're even.

JACKSON. I don't wanna be even, I want you to gimme a kiss and come home.

NOAH. I'm staying with Harper now.

JACKSON. Why'd you wanna do a thing like that?

NOAH. She wants me to.

JACKSON. And you?

NOAH. Don't matter.

JACKSON. Matters to me if you're dumping me or your sister is.

NOAH. I am.

JACKSON. Why?

NOAH. Don't gotta tell you why.

JACKSON. She treats you like a kid, like she's your momma and / she's –

NOAH. She's scared for me. 'Bout how bad it's got.

JACKSON. What, 'cause a'the game?

NOAH. *Benny* was there.

JACKSON. I know, I said we waved!

NOAH. – You knew he was there?

JACKSON. I mean Harper does her damnedest to keep me hid from him but I still know what the boy *looks* like. He's got your smile, your ears,

NOAH. You knew and you let me –

Get out.

JACKSON. Wait what? What the / hell?

NOAH. Get. *Out. Jackson.*

JACKSON. We both / saw him!

NOAH. I barely knew where the / hell I was.

JACKSON. You knew and you didn't care so don't go around acting all high and mighty like I'm the reason / you're –

NOAH. I wouldn't be hooked if it weren't for you.

JACKSON. We ain't doin' this.

NOAH. 'Cause you know I'm right, that's / why.

JACKSON. Baby, I *met* you, you were hooked!

NOAH. I was takin' my mom's Oxy, it / wasn't –

JACKSON. You wanted it so you got it from me, that my fault? We're talkin' about Williamson here, I'm not the only one could sell shit to you, only difference is mine's pure.

NOAH. Well, I can't date my dealer anymore I need to be *done* with all this.

 (Beat.)

JACKSON. All this?

 It's me, baby. I'm your Jackson.

NOAH. Stoppit.

JACKSON. I'm your big spoon. It's me you're talkin to, look at me.

NOAH. I can't, I can't do all this, I'm not in good sorts enough to –

JACKSON. Harper doesn't know how to make you happy, you barely know how, I've been workin' at it for four *years*.

NOAH. On-off, it's more like three.

JACKSON. Since we was sixteen years old, doesn't that mean somethin' to you?

NOAH. Please, quit, this / ain't what I –

JACKSON. Ain't what you want, *exactly*. Noah look at me, hold my hands, look in these eyes and tell me you don't wanna be together anymore. If that's what you really want.

NOAH. I don't have to do that.

(He takes her hands.)

JACKSON. Shit, you're freezing.

NOAH. I'm fine.

JACKSON. You're shakin', baby.

NOAH. I'm, fine.

JACKSON. You tryin to kick it cold-turkey, honeybee?

NOAH. I'm doin' it. I get clean and I can be a real part of Benny's life way I oughtta be. If I don't quit she won't let me see him.

JACKSON. Can't not let you see him, he's yours.

NOAH. Law says he's not, gave that up, you was there when I gave that up.

JACKSON. You were high as a kite when you gave that up.

NOAH. That's the whole point, Jackson.

JACKSON. What I'm sayin's maybe it didn't count when you gave him up if you weren't all there to do it. Weren't sound of mind and all that.

Maybe you could take him back if it comes to that.

(A shift.)

NOAH. You really think so?

JACKSON. I know a kid should be raised by his momma. Should see her, 't least. Very least.

NOAH. He should see me.

JACKSON. Should have a dad too. A better one than his no-show lousy piece of shit dirtbag –

NOAH. *(This is irrelevant.)* Jackson.

JACKSON. I could be his dad!

NOAH. You could maybe. Maybe you could yeah.

JACKSON. She won't let you see him if you don't break up with me?

NOAH. If I don't get clean and you're a part of that.

JACKSON. I don't do it I just sell it!

NOAH. She kinda thinks that's worse!

JACKSON. So I won't sell it to you no more if that's what you want! *You,* not Harper, screw Harper, if you want I'll cut you off / here'n now.

NOAH. Be nice, it's her home we're in.

JACKSON. This was both a y'all's home once, things had turned out a little different, this coulda been yours still. Coulda been you and me round that dinner table. So screw Harper and her home, I love you. Clean, high as a damn cloud, I don't give a shit but you wanna quit, we can make it happen. We could have a couple kids of our own, then. Could buy our own house off Cisco Drive. You and me and a house full of kids runnin' around, makin' a mess.

(*Pause.* **NOAH** *lets herself dream.*)

NOAH. And a dog?

JACKSON. Sure a dog!

NOAH. And you with your own autoshop.

JACKSON. I'll wait til NAPA goes under and buy the whole damn thing from the bastards.

NOAH. They deserve it, way they treated you.

JACKSON. And you could be manager of your own Waffle House.

NOAH. I don't – want to manage my own Waffle House, is that what you / think I want with my life? Jesus, Jackson –

JACKSON. Your own whatever! You can do anything you want, baby!

Look a'me. You're smart.

NOAH. Didn't finish high school.

JACKSON. And you're *still* this smart? Lookatchoo!

NOAH. Jackson...

JACKSON. And you're pretty. Pretty like a movie star.

NOAH. I'm not pretty like a –

JACKSON. And you're good with kids. You're *great* with kids, my nephews like you better'n they like me.

NOAH. Your nephews don't like you very much.

JACKSON. I know but they love you!

NOAH. So what're you saying?

JACKSON. I'm sayin' you're great at somethin'. We could start our future in some kinda direction.

NOAH. What about Harper, what about Benny?

JACKSON. Benny too. Picture him'n me outside playin' ball.

Can't you see our own little house? And everyone else stayin' out've our damn business and letting us be happy? Can't you see us happy?

(*Pause.*)

Gimme a chance to make us happy, honeybee.

(*He kisses her palm, then her lips. He swoops her up in his arms, she yelps and laughs. The front door opens. **HARPER** enters, arms full of groceries, kicks the door shut behind her and turns to see **NOAH** and **JACKSON**. **JACKSON** drops **NOAH**.*)

NOAH. – I was ending it, I was going to, I was doing it and and he convinced me it wasn't a good idea.

He wants me to get clean too.

JACKSON. If it's what she wants, I aim to help her.

NOAH. He won't sell to me no more. *Any* more.

JACKSON. She's gonna move back in with me.

NOAH. That we hadn't talked about, that I'm not sure about –

JACKSON. Long-term, at least.

NOAH. Once I've quit for good.

JACKSON. Main thing is we're gonna do it together.

NOAH. He's gonna help me, Harps.

He wants the same thing you do.

*(Beat. **HARPER** puts down the grocery bags.)*

HARPER. I'm gonna give you a count of ten, Jackson, because I am feeling patient today, and then I'm going to go out back and unlock the shed, and I am going to come back in here with my rifle and I am going to shoot you in the foot because I am licensed to carry in West Virginia and the law says I can shoot an intruder and you are an intruder in my home. I will not be rude to you, because I was not raised to be rude, and I will not aim to kill, but I will shoot you if you stay here because I do not allow drug dealers in my home, and certainly not my sister's drug dealer, is that clear?

JACKSON. I'm not / no intruder she let me in! She let me – Noah your sister's insane.

NOAH. Harper oh my *God* it's not an intruder it's *Jackson*.

*(**HARPER**'s countdown should overlap with* **NOAH** *and* **JACKSON**'s *lines.)*

HARPER. Ten.

NOAH. We all want the same thing, Harps, stoppit.

HARPER. Nine.

JACKSON. I ain't gonna sell to her.

HARPER. Eight.

NOAH. We wanna start a life together!

HARPER. Seven.

NOAH. I can't very well start a life off fresh like this, can I?

HARPER. Six.

NOAH. Jackson and me are gonna get *married*.

HARPER. Five.

JACKSON. Eventually, not right away.

HARPER. Four.

NOAH. When I get clean we're gonna get married and –

HARPER. Three.

NOAH. And Jackson's gonna get to know Benny and –

HARPER. Over my dead body, two.

JACKSON. You're gonna need me if you want her clean.

> *(Short beat.)*

You need someone on your side who knows the drug *and* knows her.

I could teach you 'bout it! I can tell you what her eyes look like when she's used an hour ago, the way she gets when she needs it, I know what signs to look out for and when, I know the places she does it. That's some use t'this, ain't it?

Could help you help her get better, couldn't I?

*(**HARPER** is silent.)*

NOAH. You want me to get better.

HARPER. Yes.

NOAH. So no gun.

JACKSON. She was gonna *shoot* me.

HARPER. Shut up.

NOAH. We can make a plan.

HARPER. Had a plan. Step number one of the plan was to break up with Jackson.

NOAH. Us three can make a new plan. Better this way. Between the two of y'all you know me all the way, I couldn't hide nothing from *both* of you.

JACKSON. She has a point.

HARPER. *(Without punch to it.)* Shut up.

(Beat.)

Noah stays here, that's not changing.

JACKSON. If that's what she wants.

HARPER. Noah stays here.

NOAH. Okay.

JACKSON. Fine.

HARPER. I don't want Jackson under the same roof as Benny.

NOAH. Then where'll I see him?

HARPER. He can – come here once a week, at a time I agree to, when Benny isn't home and when I am.

JACKSON. She ain't a kid!

HARPER. This is for now, and I'm being generous.

NOAH. Yes okay.

JACKSON. Noah!

NOAH. Better than breaking up.

HARPER. If I hear you are carrying drugs when you come
here.

If I hear you offer to sell to Noah ever again.

If I hear you do business in my home.

JACKSON. Whatever, okay.

HARPER. I will take that rifle and I will shoot you. And not
in the foot. Do I make myself clear?

Scene Three

*(The next afternoon. **HARPER** is in her pajamas, cleaning the house. Over the sound of the vacuum, she doesn't hear knocking on the door. The knocks become louder. **HARPER** notices, turns off the vacuum. She slowly moves the vacuum to the side, walks toward the door.)*

AUBREY. *(Offstage.)* Is Noah Attridge there?

*(**HARPER** stops, considers. She looks through the keyhole, puts on a sweater over her pajamas, opens the door. **AUBREY** stands in the doorway holding a clipboard and a handbag.)*

Is this the residence of Noah Attridge?

HARPER. – Is anything wrong?

AUBREY. Oh, no, nothing's –

You're not in any trouble, but I am hoping to have a conversation with –

HARPER. How did you get this address?

AUBREY. Y'know, I just asked. People around here – well, you've got a small town. Small town charm! Do people say that, about Williamson?

HARPER. They do not.

AUBREY. Well –

Listen, I know you've been in some trouble as of late but I'm not here to judge, and I'm not here to –

HARPER. Some trouble?

AUBREY. I mean, you must have seen the article, the, it was trending for a couple days there –

HARPER. In this small town of ours, when we knock on a stranger's door, we get to the point around why.

AUBREY. I'm doing a lousy job of this, I'm sorry, I drove a good six hours to get here, to be honest, so I'm all over the place, and on top of that I'm new-ish to the job, to the fieldwork side of things, but I'll get to my point, I'm sure you're very busy, with – I'm Aubrey. *Hi.* I'm here on behalf of an organization called Project Protection, and we work with women suffering from addiction. We look to give them more options. We know it can feel like there are little to no options.

Noah, I'm here to tell you – to promise you – that you have options.

HARPER. I'm not Noah.

AUBREY. Honey, you can – anything you say to me is confidential, strictly. You can be real with me.

HARPER. Oh, I can be real with you?

AUBREY. One hundred percent.

HARPER. Oh, good. Noah's my sister, that was my sister in the article, and she's not here. And I do not use. You want to write that down?

AUBREY. Your sister. Oh! The article didn't mention –

HARPER. What *specific* business are you here for, Aubrey?

AUBREY. So, like I was saying, the organization I'm representing provides resources for–

HARPER. You drove six hours to "provide resources for" my sister?

AUBREY. The short answer is yes. I'd like to give you the long answer, but just for the sake of your family's privacy, we might want to have that conversation inside.

Or I can wait to just speak to Noah directly. If you'd rather not be involved.

(**HARPER** *weighs her options, exhales. She steps aside.*)

HARPER. Shoes off.

AUBREY. Sure, sure. Thank you, really.

(*She steps in past* **HARPER** *and takes in the home.*)

You've got a lovely –

HARPER. Thanks. You can get right to it.

AUBREY. So, well, okay. I heard about your sister's story, I read about it, and – usually, I stick to a two-hour radius max for work, but her story touched me. Really. I feel drawn to, more than anything, to helping young women in crisis. I read the article and I thought – respectfully – this person needs help. From someone who gets it, who cares.

HARPER. Right.

Here's the thing – respectfully – you don't know my sister. You don't know anything about our lives / beyond –

AUBREY. No, you're right, no, but that story made me think about people in my own life who've struggled, who've needed help and haven't asked for it – it made me think about my daughter, actually, and –

Like I said, I'm new to the fieldwork. I don't know if it's inappropriate, telling you all of this, but my daughter is an addict. So I have a personal connection to all this. And for the last few years, I've tried to do something about it. I started volunteering at a shelter for homeless addicts, but it...it didn't feel like we were giving those people futures. We weren't breaking the cycle, we were just delaying it a little. And that was best-case scenario. I wanted to do more. So this is me trying to do more. Doing it poorly, I guess. They would've sent someone with more experience, and someone, well, a bit closer by, but I told them, I want this case, I feel connected to –

HARPER. My sister is a case?

AUBREY. Well, so, only if she chooses to be. I'm just here to offer help to your sister. I can't imagine it's been easy for anyone involved, especially with – well, the article mentioned she has a child –

HARPER. *(Alert.)* Benny?

AUBREY. Is that –? Gosh, what a sweet name.

HARPER. Benny is not in my sister's custody. He's in mine. So he doesn't need help.

AUBREY. Oh, how great. It sounds like he's lucky, then. But – still – I know that children of drug addicts can have their own range of difficulties, regardless of who's taking care of them. Does he, say, experience any symptoms of NAS? Sorry, that's neonatal abstinence / syndrome –

HARPER. No, I know what NAS is, he – yeah, he had it.

AUBREY. And what does that look like now?

I know most kids with NAS can barely go fifteen seconds without losing focus, so.

HARPER. ...He has ADHD.

AUBREY. Trouble sleeping? Hard times with goodbyes, even temporary ones? Seizures, occasionally?

HARPER. Uh. All of those, yes.

AUBREY. It's brutal, right? How old was your sister when he was born? If you don't mind me / asking.

HARPER. Honestly, I still don't entirely understand what you're here for.

AUBREY. You don't trust me, I get it, I'm a stranger from out of town and I just showed up out of the blue and –

I'm sorry, what's your name?

HARPER. – Harper.

AUBREY. Harper. Harper, listen, I'm already bending some confidentiality requirements to talk to you with your sister not present, which is – my fault, not yours – so I'm gonna save the nitty-gritty of all this for when I get the chance to talk to Noah, but the short story is that I work to help women in circumstances outside of their control regain that control. We would work together, based on your sister's needs. I'm just someone looking to help.

And in the meantime, the least I can do is listen. I know there have been times in my life when I really could've used someone, someone who understood, to just listen.

(Pause.)

I can come back another time, if –

HARPER. She was fifteen, almost sixteen. When Benny was born.

AUBREY. – Oh, *young,* gosh. And you've been taking care of them both ever since?

HARPER. I've… I've had custody since Benny was six months old, I mean officially, but Noah was never – I mean she was still a kid, when he –

AUBREY. Of course.

HARPER. She had high school, she had –

AUBREY. Fifteen.

HARPER. Right. But she moved out at seventeen, so. She's taken care of herself since then.

AUBREY. Independent! Wow.

HARPER. Well, it wasn't – entirely her decision, she'd relapsed, after this long period of – her longest, I guess, of sobriety, and I couldn't have her around –

AUBREY. Benny, right, of course.

HARPER. So she's lived with her boyfriend, mostly, since. Till now.

AUBREY. That period of sobriety, how long was –?

HARPER. Nine months, almost ten. Our mom had just OD'd, so – wake-up call, all that.

AUBREY. Ah, your mother was a user.

HARPER. Of OxyContin, not – but yeah.

AUBREY. These generational cycles. Hard to break.

HARPER. I don't know about cycles. She got in a car crash, never stopped taking what they gave her afterward. Noah, she'd take pills with her friends like some kids take whiskey from their parents' liquor cabinets, it wasn't like they were the same.

AUBREY. You've had to take care of a lot of people.

> (**AUBREY**'s gaze lands on a nearby picture of Benny.)

Is this –?

HARPER. That's him.

AUBREY. Oh he is *precious*.

Oh look at those cheeks. That *smile*.

HARPER. He's got my sister's smile.

AUBREY. You two have the same eyes, though. Wow, it's striking.

HARPER. I don't know.

AUBREY. He's lucky to have you. You seem like a great mom.

HARPER. Well, guardian.

AUBREY. Guardian, right, sorry. Just – do you plan to transfer care back to your sister at any point?

HARPER. I, no.

AUBREY. And you said you've raised him all by yourself?

HARPER. I have.

AUBREY. Huh. Sounds like a mom to me.

(Pause.)

HARPER. Just to be clear – Benny's not a burden. To me or to Noah. And Noah, actually, she's decided she wants to get clean. Do it right this time.

AUBREY. Oh! That must be a recent development.

HARPER. Yeah, it's only been a few days, but –

AUBREY. Right, since the – sorry, you said she's out of the house?

HARPER. Well, right now, she's at work.

AUBREY. Stop me if I'm overstepping, but I assume you're checking her location every ten, fifteen minutes?

HARPER. I'm – not, she doesn't have a smartphone.

AUBREY. A tracker, then?

HARPER. I wouldn't even know where to get one of those, not in Williamson.

AUBREY. Do you have her boss's number?

HARPER. I – no.

AUBREY. Huh. Have you been checking her arms every night, her legs, her feet, her belly, even? Her pupils?

HARPER. No, okay, no, but this isn't the first time we've done this. The last time she promised to get clean, she did. For nine months, like I / said.

AUBREY. But at some point she'd been clean for all that time and she still slipped up, right? And then it was zero days. And now it's been a few days. It's a hill you don't stop climbing, unfortunately. I'm not here to scare you and say your sister's definitely out there getting high right now, or planning to. I'm just saying you'd have no way of knowing if she was.

HARPER. Look, you don't know my sister.

AUBREY. Of course. But addiction is more formulaic than you'd think. Addicts' behavior may seem random, but in some ways, it's not at all.

She probably said that this time would be different, right? Accused you of not trusting her, believing in her? Made you feel like if you gave up on her, there'd be no point in her trying to get clean at all.

I've heard all the lines. Heard them, believed them, heard them again.

Maybe I'm wrong, but.

(Pause.)

HARPER. I should get her boss's number.

AUBREY. Just a suggestion. I have more, if you're open to hearing them.

Scene Four

*(The next night. **NOAH** is washing dishes – mostly just rinsing them and putting them on a rack or towel to dry. She hums as she works. She stops, noticing a sound from Benny's room – **HARPER** is singing a lullaby offstage. She pauses, keeps washing dishes. A bout of nausea hits. She keels over, breathes hard. **HARPER** enters from the hallway, closes the door behind her quietly.)*

HARPER. Asleep, finally.

Oh. Are you gonna –?

NOAH. Nope. Just gimme a,

HARPER. Okay.

*(**NOAH** drops to her knees, keeps breathing. **HARPER** watches her.)*

NOAH. Can you stop.

HARPER. Stop –

NOAH. Looking at me?

*(**HARPER** starts doing the dishes, picking up where **NOAH** left off. The bout eases up.)*

I can keep doin' em.

HARPER. It's fine, you don't wash them right anyway.

NOAH. No wrong way to wash dishes.

HARPER. I'm gonna disagree with you there.

NOAH. I'm tryin to / help out around the –!

HARPER. *(Amused.)* Well, you're not gonna be helping out by getting sick everywhere, so –

NOAH. It'll pass. Only threw up once today.

HARPER. You sure you can work, feeling like this?

NOAH. Work helps. Keeps me too busy to think about it.

HARPER. About the nausea?

NOAH. About drugs.

HARPER. I was gonna offer you an aspirin for your stomach but maybe that's not a good idea.

NOAH. It's heroin I want, Harper, I don't think aspirin's gonna be an issue.

> (*Pause.* **HARPER** *starts to laugh.* **NOAH** *joins in.*)

You can't laugh at heroin jokes.

HARPER. I've earned it. By association, strictly.

Y'know I've never done a single drug in my life?

NOAH. Well, good, I've got you beat at one thing.

HARPER. Psh. You've beat me at plenty.

NOAH. Like what?

HARPER. You always had more friends!

NOAH. That don't count.

HARPER. It counts, it counts.

Mom liked you better.

NOAH. That ain't true.

HARPER. Don't play dumb, you were her baby.

NOAH. I don't know.

HARPER. You do so know.

NOAH. Maybe a little bit.

But I always thought she liked your daddy better.

HARPER. She hated yours and mine, the both of 'em.

NOAH. Hated yours less though!

HARPER. ...Maybe a little bit.

NOAH. Uh huh.

I felt bad for her. I think that's why I could never get mad. I just felt so bad for her.

HARPER. I didn't. Made every decision got her where she was.

NOAH. Here we go with the...

HARPER. What?

NOAH. You can just. Be a lil judgy is all.

HARPER. Excuse me!

NOAH. That can't be *news* t'you.

HARPER. If I was judgy I would've –

NOAH. What?

HARPER. Well! Said a lot to you that I haven't!

(*The shortest pause.*)

NOAH. Ohoho / hold up.

HARPER. No, we're not doin' this,

NOAH. What've you held back from sayin to me?

HARPER. I'm just saying. That if I were looking for things to judge I'd have no shortage of those things but I'm not / *looking*!

NOAH. Buuuulllllshiiiiit.

HARPER. Noah –!

NOAH. Bullcrap, sorry!

(*She waits for* **HARPER**, *who says nothing, just dries the dishes.*)

NOAH. *(Teasing.)* I think you don't know how to dress as good as you could.

HARPER. What?

NOAH. That's something I judge about you. I've held back from saying it.

HARPER. I don't like this. I don't wanna fight.

NOAH. It's not fighting! It's a game!

HARPER. I don't like games.

NOAH. Oh I know! You know I took out Candy Land and Benny said he'd never *played before?*

HARPER. We're missing some pieces. Pieces you lost, if I remember –

NOAH. What *do* you play, then? Kid's gotta have fun sometime!

HARPER. You can make jokes about my clothes but not about how I raise Benny.

NOAH. You're so *serious.*

(*Pause.*)

HARPER. There's a puzzle I think, in the back of the closet. You can do that with him.

NOAH. That what y'all do?

HARPER. No, he hasn't seen it yet,

NOAH. It's new?

HARPER. Yeah, it's not a big deal. Like you said, I don't like games anyway.

NOAH. Look at you bein' all nice.

(**NOAH** *teasingly reaches out for her sister's hand.* **HARPER** *shoos her away.*)

HARPER. Quit.

NOAH. My biiig sister, takin' care of me.

HARPER. Okay, okay.

> *(Abruptly, a wave of nausea hits hard.*
> ***NOAH*** *twists away. Beat.)*

NOAH. I should go lie down before my stomach gets all...
yeah.

> *(She starts to leave the kitchen.* ***HARPER***
> *decides to humor her:)*

HARPER. You have bad taste in men.

NOAH. What?

HARPER. I was – the game, I was trying to play –

> *(Still nauseous but bouncing back delightedly:)*

NOAH. You got no taste in men and no friends cause you're
always here or at work.

HARPER. You...act less smart than you really are so people
don't take you as seriously as they could.

NOAH. You're bossy.

HARPER. I am not! Am I?

NOAH. Oh my Lord, Harps, yes.

HARPER. You curse too much.

NOAH. You can't take a joke. You've never been able to
take a joke.

HARPER. Alright, we're done.

NOAH. (What'd I say.)

HARPER. By the way, I have friends.

NOAH. Okay, I just don't know them!

HARPER. I work with them! It's tame, maybe, but it's good, we joke about our least favorite students in the teacher's lounge and Lori Holden brings homemade apple cake and it's y'know it's pretty bad but we all eat it anyway. I don't need to go out and make a fool of myself to have fun. Not that – I'm not saying that's what you do.

Okay now that I'm listening for it maybe I'm. A little judgy.

NOAH. You could stand to go out was all I meant.

HARPER. Go out? What town do you live in?

NOAH. There's Dandy's!

HARPER. *Dandy's.* Gross.

NOAH. I just don't want you to be lonely!

HARPER. I don't have enough free time on my hands to get lonely.

NOAH. Yeah.

I get pretty lonely.

HARPER. You do?

NOAH. Yeah.

HARPER. I'm sorry.

NOAH. Naw. Just.

You know. I got too many dead friends.

HARPER. I know.

NOAH. Less lonely stayin' here though. If you'd let me spend more time with Benny and you I'd barely be –

HARPER. We'll work up to it.

NOAH. Right.

(Beat.)

HARPER. Maybe a change could help.

NOAH. Change'a what?

HARPER. Something. Job, maybe.

NOAH. Cause Williamson's got so many of those.

HARPER. Place, then.

NOAH. *(Hurt but hiding it.)* You tryna get rid of me?

HARPER. No, I just want you to think about your future.

(Beat. They finish doing dishes.)

NOAH. Actually. Jackson and me, we always talked about. If I ever stayed clean and all that, we always wanted to start a family. We got a list of baby names on his phone and everything.

So that could be / a change.

HARPER. Like kids, having kids?

NOAH. Yup. Brothers and sisters for Benny, so.

HARPER. – Oh.

NOAH. What does oh mean.

HARPER. It's just quick, it's just kinda *soon* I guess to / hear you say –

NOAH. You're the one said I needed a change, needed to think about my *future*.

HARPER. I meant I could help you look for a new job, or take a class at Southern Tech, not –!

NOAH. We don't want the same stuff, Harp!

HARPER. Obviously not, but –

NOAH. Just 'cause you think what I want is dumb doesn't mean it's dumb to me.

(Beat. The comfort between them is gone.)

NOAH. *(Flat.)* Remember when Benny was born?

HARPER. Of course I do.

NOAH. It all happened so fast. Those first few months, the agreements we made. Always thought I'd get him back, y'know, at some point. When I was old enough, or.

HARPER. Fast or not, you agreed it was the best thing, you signed the custody papers.

NOAH. Well, I wasn't right of mind when I signed them.

HARPER. And doesn't that just go to show why you didn't get him back?

NOAH. I'm right of mind now!

HARPER. For now you are, yes.

> *(The shortest of pauses.)*

NOAH. You think I / won't –

HARPER. I don't think anything.

NOAH. For *now* you said, you don't think I'll be / able to –

HARPER. I think it's been four days, Noah!

NOAH. Fine.

HARPER. It's just –

NOAH. I SAID FINE LET'S DROP IT.

> *(Crying from the other room.* **HARPER** *turns to look,* **NOAH** *covers her mouth.)*

I didn't mean to.

> *(***HARPER** *goes toward Benny's room.)*

I can help, I can –

HARPER. You stay put, I'll tend to him.

NOAH. I'm sorry, I didn't –

*(**NOAH** tries to follow but keels over in pain as another bout of nausea hits. **HARPER** stops, sees.)*

HARPER. Noah.

NOAH. I'm fine, go.

Please go.

*(**HARPER** goes. **NOAH** recovers, with effort. She listens as the crying grows quiet.)*

Scene Five

*(The next day. **NOAH** sits at the table, snacking. Her withdrawals are visibly worsening: she's agitated, anxious, achy in her skin. **AUBREY** is taking off her shoes.)*

AUBREY. I was so glad you called. Any excuse to get out of that motel, really, is a (ha) welcome one.

I think I'm the only guest, as a matter of fact.

NOAH. That motel's haunted as shit.

HARPER. Cursing jar, Noah.

*(**NOAH**, mouth full of snacks, waves.)*

NOAH. I'm Noah.

(She drops a quarter into a newly labeled jar on the table.)

AUBREY. Hi! Aubrey! It's nice to –

NOAH. Oh you're not from here.

AUBREY. People keep saying that.

NOAH. *(Bored.)* Who is she?

HARPER. She's someone who's here to help.

AUBREY. Can I sit at the table with you?

NOAH. Ain't my house.

HARPER. Of course you can, I'll, uh.

You want something to eat, drink? We've got water or tea.

AUBREY. Herbal?

HARPER. Sweet.

AUBREY. I'm good, thanks, we can just, sit and chat.

NOAH. What'd'you mean she's here to help?

HARPER. Let's be polite, Noah.

NOAH. I'm just askin'.

AUBREY. And it's a reasonable question! I came by the other day to, well, I was looking for you, but I found Harper, and we talked and talked and – I hope it was useful –

HARPER. It was, very.

AUBREY. – and I asked her if I could meet with you and she said she'd think about it and –

NOAH. Lucky me.

HARPER. She works with addicts.

AUBREY. Female addicts.

NOAH. Cat's out of the bag, huh.

AUBREY. Oh, she didn't, uh. I read an article, a couple, actually, about the uh –

NOAH. Great.

AUBREY. But I could've – and please don't take this in a bad way –

NOAH. I'm listenin'.

AUBREY. *(As politely as possible.)* I could've recognized you as an addict without the article.

NOAH. Gee, Harps, you got some sweet friends.

AUBREY. It must sound – sorry – I'm just, between personal experience and my field of work, I know how to recognize –

NOAH. What exactly is that field?

AUBREY. I'm a representative for Project Protection.

NOAH. I never heard of y'all.

AUBREY. We work with female addicts who have had or are considering having more children.

HARPER. She wants to help provide resources for us.

NOAH. Like money?

AUBREY. There is a cash incentive aspect to what we do, yes.

NOAH. Cash, nice.

HARPER. Do we need to apply for some kind of loan / or –

AUBREY. No no, no application necessary,

NOAH. Free cash!

HARPER. I thought you were offering subsidized Narcan or – I don't know, rehab services –

AUBREY. Right, no, we're – that stuff is all great, believe me, but – we stay a little more focused in our mission.

NOAH. What's your "mission?"

(**AUBREY** *inhales, exhales –*)

AUBREY. As of this month, we've successfully provided nearly eight thousand addicts with permanent birth control, and through the generosity of donors from all around the country, we're equipped with the resources to compensate them for the operation in question.

(*Beat.*)

HARPER. Permanent birth control?

AUBREY. So, tubal ligation, is the specific – it's a minimally invasive –

HARPER. You *sterilize* people?

AUBREY. Well, I think that word is a little –

NOAH. You can go to hell, and you can go with her.

HARPER. Noah, this is news to me.

NOAH. Like hell it is, I tell you me and Jackson wanna start a family when I've been clean for a while and you call up your friend and say hey come on over and *fix* her like a goddamn *dog*.

AUBREY. Harper and I did not discuss the specifics of my organization.

HARPER. I called her because I realized I might need help to help you better. If I'd known she was peddling some kinda new-edition Mississippi appendectomy –

AUBREY. Listen, I know how it sounds at first.

HARPER. It sounds like you bribe addicts / to get –

AUBREY. No no, it's all purely voluntary. The cash incentive makes it more attractive, but –

NOAH. How do y'all know I wouldn't go and use your *cash incentive* to re-up?

AUBREY. We don't. All parts of the process rely on the free will of our clients. It would be coercive, otherwise.

HARPER. It's coercive as is. They're addicts, they're not thinking straight.

NOAH. I can talk for myself. I'm getting clean, you tell her that?

AUBREY. She did, and I think it's great you're trying.

And – I know this all sounds a little intense. When you first hear it. But the reality is that we live in a country that isn't yet equipped to care for people struggling with addiction, let alone help those in the path of, ah. Destruction's not exactly the right word –

HARPER. This is not sounding any less intense.

AUBREY. And, and, most people don't know this, addiction is fifty percent attributed to genetic predisposition, okay? And the children of addicts are eight times more likely to develop an addiction of their own so, *so* it's one part of the problem we can address.

HARPER. One part of the –

AUBREY. It's not the *only* solution, it's not a *perfect* solution, sure, but it's *a* solution. To kids being raised with disadvantages they had no part in causing. Harper, you yourself said Benny has challenges.

HARPER. I'm gonna ask you to keep Benny out of this.

Sorry to waste your time, but we're not interested.

AUBREY. *(A last-ditch effort.)* Harper mentioned on the phone that you're dating your drug dealer.

HARPER. I –

NOAH. Harper!

AUBREY. I want you to think about how exactly you're going to get clean and start a family with him, while he still has the product. While he's still in the world you're trying to get out of, right?

NOAH. You don't know.

AUBREY. With due respect, my –

My daughter is a heroin addict. I do know.

NOAH. She get the operation?

AUBREY. She did not.

NOAH. So she could be out there with more kids'n me, then.

AUBREY. My daughter is dead.

But, no, she did not get it before.

But she was also – clean, for five years, before she. It's reserved for active users, so.

NOAH. Seems kinda fucked to only offer it to someone who you know's not thinking straight.

AUBREY. And to me I guess it seems shortsighted and selfish to expose a baby to opioids and raise him in an unsafe environment.

NOAH. Benny's safe.

AUBREY. And you haven't raised him.

With all due respect.

> *(Beat. **AUBREY** slides a pamphlet across the table to **NOAH**.)*

This has all the information, the statistics of our business.

Six thousand of our clients' living children are out of their custody, in foster care. That's two times the population of this whole town.

Then, there's – eight hundred stillborns. Five hundred babies dying shortly after birth.

In an ideal world, we'd be able to do more for everyone involved. It's just that right now no one's being helped, so.

> *(She waits for a reaction and gets none.)*

The pamphlet also describes the financial compensation you'd receive. The um, the money.

NOAH. I know. What compensation means.

> *(**NOAH** opens the pamphlet, glances at it. Pause. She looks at **HARPER**, then at **AUBREY**. She drops the pamphlet on the table, collects her things and moves for the door.)*

AUBREY. Just think about it.

NOAH. *(Without punch to it.)* Go to hell.

HARPER. You'll be done at nine?

NOAH. Yep.

(*To* **AUBREY**.) I'm not just *tryin'*. I'm doin' it. Been doin' it five days. You don't know.

AUBREY. – I wish you the best of luck.

> (**NOAH** *leaves the house, slamming the door behind her.*)

HARPER. You need to leave too.

AUBREY. I'm sorry if I caught you off-guard, but I just want to / help.

HARPER. Yeah, I'm actually good.

AUBREY. You're just going to keep being put in the same position. Raising her kids, kids with challenges.

HARPER. I told you Benny is not a burden.

AUBREY. And I heard you, I hear you. But what about six Bennys? And what about when she relapses and you have to take care of her, too?

Your sister's choices shouldn't always have to be your responsibility. That's all I'm saying.

> (**AUBREY** *packs up her things.* **HARPER** *won't look at her. Beat.*)

It seems like you'd do pretty much anything for your family. I get it, I'm the same way. But don't think you're doing her a favor by expecting her to change overnight.

My Charlotte relapsed after five years. Five – *years*, and I still wonder what I could've –

It never ends, so.

> (*Beat.* **AUBREY** *taps the pamphlet.*)

For when you change your mind, okay?

*(She leaves. **HARPER** stares at the table for a long moment. She reaches for the pamphlet.)*

Scene Six

*(Much later that night. **HARPER** is pacing, waiting for **NOAH** to come home. She picks up some toys left on the floor, smooths the blanket on the couch. A sound at the front door, and **NOAH** walks in. Her entire body aches; she's muscling through it.)*

HARPER. You're home late.

NOAH. Walked home.

HARPER. I could've given you a ride.

NOAH. No need.

HARPER. Well, I had to stay up and wait.

NOAH. Didn't have to.

HARPER. I need to know you're home and safe.

NOAH. I walk home from work plenty. Ain't been murdered yet.

HARPER. You seemed upset when you left, I was worried –

NOAH. Worried I'd what?

HARPER. Noah.

NOAH. You treat me like I'm a bomb about to go off. You think that helps? It don't help.

HARPER. Just, give me a call next time you're walking home.

NOAH. Great. Gimme a call next time you wanna get my tubes tied for cash.

HARPER. I told you, I didn't know what Aubrey –

NOAH. Stupid name.

HARPER. I didn't know.

NOAH. You told her about Jackson.

HARPER. I...

You're right. I'm sorry.

>	*(Beat. With effort:)*

I have – a hard time being helped.

She seemed like she had help to give. It's not like there's a handbook to all this, I don't know what I'm doing any more than...

I feel pretty stupid now, so.

NOAH. You're not stupid.

Nosy know-it-all, maybe, but not stupid.

HARPER. Thanks.

NOAH. Pushy control freak, maybe, but –

HARPER. Alright, alright.

>	*(A tentative shift between them. **NOAH** takes
>	a deep breath.)*

NOAH. There was this one day when – you remember that heat wave, when I was...five or six? You woulda been ten.

HARPER. I remember.

NOAH. Well, you were at school, I wasn't old enough yet, and Mom was somewhere, work I guess,

And it was just about June, and it was already so hot I thought I'd die. I'd been sucking on ice cubes and keeping the fridge open with my face in it, but I knew Mom would get mad at me for wasting.

And I went out and checked the mail, don't know why, just felt hopeful,

NOAH. And there was this flyer from this air conditioning company. BUY TODAY, in huge letters. It was all blue, with snowflakes or icicles or somethin going across it, and it had the phone number underneath. And a picture of a girl with the air going in her face, looking so happy.

And I was feelin' brave, or spiteful, or somethin', that all the fans we had weren't doing crap but taking hot air and blowing it right back at us, and you got to be at school in a nice cool classroom and here I was stuck in my own sweat, and I took the home phone and called the number, made my voice a lil deeper, and I ordered an air conditioner.

It was a hundred fifty dollars. One forty-nine ninety-nine.

Mom had her credit card in her nightstand, and I went and took it and read the numbers.

And I knew I'd done something bad, even while I was doin it.

But I thought maybe – maybe – Mom would understand. Or be happy I'd done it. She didn't like the heat either.

And it took three weeks and I don't think I slept once in those three weeks, and then it showed up on our doorstep and Mom looked at it and said, there musta been some kind of mistake.

And then she looked at me and I must have looked guilty as sin, cause she looked at me for a long time without saying a word and then she went and called the credit card company. And I thought she was gonna whoop me so bad. But she just told them, all calm, there must have been some kind of mistake, and she'd be returning it.

She sorted it all out on the phone. Didn't even open the box. Brought it to the post office the next day and it was gone. And when she got home, she went to her room and took the fan in there and brought it into our room. Do you remember, when all of a sudden we had two fans?

HARPER. I do.

NOAH. And I was cryin', following her, and sayin' how sorry I was, and she didn't have to do that, she needed that fan more'n we did, and she didn't even look at me, she just plugged it in, went back to her room, shut the door.

The second fan helped a little, on the hottest days. Felt sick to my stomach every time it did.

HARPER. You never told me all that.

NOAH. Never came up.

HARPER. She shouldn't have left you alone in the heat.

She could've brought you to work, or dropped you at the church for day care.

NOAH. She did the best she could.

Anyway, it's just a memory. Came to me all of a sudden.

(Beat. Another shift between them.)

HARPER. I'm gonna need some help with Benny.

NOAH. I can play with him. Or, take him to school –

HARPER. No, I mean – he has some challenges. Behavioral, learning, uh. He needs therapy, he might even need to go to an out-of-district school next year, is what his Pre-K teacher thinks.

NOAH. Thought he was gonna be in your class next year.

HARPER. I did too. I'm not so sure. He's a bright kid, just. He needs more support than he's getting, right now.

NOAH. What are you askin' me.

HARPER. I'm not –

NOAH. Be honest.

HARPER. – Noah, I can't afford another kid.

NOAH. I never said you were getting one.

Did *Aubrey* tell you you were getting another –

HARPER. She just raised some questions. Questions I should've considered without her having to ask them.

NOAH. You want me to do it.

HARPER. That's not what I'm saying.

NOAH. You didn't say no.

(Beat.)

I, uh. Got Employee of the Week. They put my picture up today.

HARPER. Oh. / Noah, that's –

NOAH. It's Waffle House, it's stupid, it doesn't matter.

HARPER. Of course it matters.

NOAH. It's been everyone but me for years so I guess they had to get around to me at some point.

HARPER. I'm proud of you.

NOAH. There's no prize or anything, I asked.

HARPER. Still. Congratulations.

*(**NOAH** looks at her feet.)*

NOAH. I'll read the pamphlet once and then we're never talking about it again.

HARPER. Okay.

NOAH. Having kids could make me have to be better.

I'm doing good with Benny. I did that puzzle with him this mornin' and he liked it. He really liked it. Said there's not always a lot of playin' happens around here, so.

>   *(Pause.)*

HARPER. It's late, get some sleep. You need a ride to work tomorrow?

Scene Seven

(The next evening. Benny is in his room; **NOAH** *is at work.* **JACKSON** *and* **HARPER** *sit on opposite sides of the dining table, a pitcher of sweet tea between them. Silence as he drains a glass. As he places it down:)*

HARPER. Right, then. So,

JACKSON. Tea's real good, Harps.

HARPER. Don't call me Harps.

JACKSON. Noah calls you Harps!

HARPER. You're not family.

JACKSON. Not yet, anyway!

HARPER. *(Ignoring that.)* So the reason I asked you here.

JACKSON. You're tired of her sleepin' here? She snores like a woman twice her age, I'll give y'that much, I'll take her back / in with –

HARPER. No, Noah stays put.

JACKSON. She hasn't used since last week. *Or* asked to cop any, I'd have told you.

HARPER. Good, I mean that's all good, but –

Jackson, you care about my sister?

JACKSON. Course I do. Like a fool I do.

HARPER. Enough to stop selling? Not just to her, I mean at all.

JACKSON. Uh... I got laid off months ago from NAPA. I gotta eat. 'N so does my brother Jason, can't work on account of his Iraq leg.

HARPER. You were selling before your job there.

JACKSON. It's the best money I can make in Mingo County, let alone Williamson. I don't know what t'tell you, you know about jobs here. The Economy, all that. Ain't what it was.

Way I see it, they'll get it somewhere else if they don't get it from me, and from me they get it cleaner, and I don't sell in bulk, and it ain't from a junkie. I tell the folks I sell to what they can handle and can't.

HARPER. Could Noah get it from somewhere else? Does she know anyone?

JACKSON. She don't know the others, ain't many close by. Might've heard some names but she don't know how to get to'm.

HARPER. What about the rest of Mingo County?

JACKSON. She's here or at work! Ain't driving through the whole county lookin'.

HARPER. You don't know that.

JACKSON. I do know that.

HARPER. 'Cause you trust her?

JACKSON. No, 'cause I know her! And I love her, and she loves me just's much. She wouldn't buy from no one else but me.

HARPER. You say it like it's sweet.

JACKSON. I just know her is all. Know what she'd do and wouldn't. Don't you?

> (*The door opens.* **NOAH** *enters, exhausted, in a Waffle House apron and hat.*[*] *She puts down her things and sees* **JACKSON.**)

---

[*] A license to produce *Spay* does not include a license to publicly display any branded logos or trademarked images. Licensees must acquire rights for any logos and/or images or create their own.

NOAH. Baby, what're you –?

JACKSON. – Surprise!

> (**HARPER** *stays seated.* **JACKSON** *gets up and gives* **NOAH** *a big hug, kisses her palm.*)

Harper thought we could all eat dinner together. Like a family!

HARPER. *(Low.)* Oh, I didn't say that.

NOAH. Harper, you did this for me? You really did this for me?

JACKSON. Your hair smells like bacon.

NOAH. Oh shit, *shoot,* does it?

JACKSON. I like it.

NOAH. Jackson loves food, all food. Loves it. Once we had a fight and he came to work and ordered so much stuff so he could keep talking to me till we made up.

JACKSON. I ordered so much stuff.

NOAH. He got like six different combos I don't even know how he did it.

JACKSON. Couldn't even look at waffles for a week.

HARPER. Okay let's eat dinner. Jackson can stay another half hour.

NOAH. Wait could Benny meet –?!

HARPER. He's in his room and staying there, I gave him dinner before. Workin' on your puzzle.

NOAH. *(To* **JACKSON**.*)* He likes puzzles now.

But next time maybe?

HARPER. We'll work up to maybe.

NOAH. This is good. This makes me *happy!*

HARPER. Go on and change, Jackson'll help me with the food.

NOAH. Be nice, everyone?

(**NOAH** *leaves the room.*)

HARPER. I need something from you.

JACKSON. Okay,

HARPER. I need all the names. All the people, all the addresses I could go to if she doesn't come home on time one day.

JACKSON. *(Laughing.)* You want a list of every drop-off spot in Mingo County?

HARPER. That's exactly what I want, and you're gonna make it before Noah comes back in, so start.

(**HARPER** *takes out a pen and a piece of paper.* **JACKSON** *scribbles down a few names and addresses and hands over the paper.*)

JACKSON. You treat your kids this way, all bossy like that?

HARPER. I treat children like children, if that's what you're asking.

JACKSON. (This why you don't have a boyfriend, huh.)

HARPER. You wanna say that a little louder?

JACKSON. I could fix you up with my cousin Jim on my mom's side. Ain't all that much to look at but he's sure nice. Me'n Noah could take Benny off your hands and you could live your own life for –

HARPER. *(Level.)* Me raising Benny is not some kind of temporary situation, and you are never going to be a part of his life.

JACKSON. He's Noah's kid, ain't he? I could be his step-daddy.

HARPER. You shut your god-damn mouth.

    (Beat.)

JACKSON. You know somethin, Harper? You put me down time and time again, in front of Noah, to my face and everything, and I don't say a word. I don't say nothin' unkind back to you, nothin' disrespectful. But you try a man's last nerve, alright? I'm, listen. I'm not some idiot and I'm not uncaring and I'm not a bad person. I'm good. I try to be good. And I am always good to your sister, as good as I know how. She could do worse, okay? I ain't perfect but she could – I try to be good. So just, so just, dangit,

Can't we be civil, 'tleast? For Noah's sake?

    (Beat. **NOAH** *reenters, face washed and clothes changed, feeling feverish but smiling through it.)*

NOAH. You helpin' out my sister, Jackson?

JACKSON. Tryin' to.

HARPER. *(With great reluctance.)* You can set the table.

JACKSON. I'm on it.

HARPER. But wash your hands first, I don't need help from hands looking like those.

    *(***HARPER*** *heads to Benny's room as* **JACKSON** *washes his hands and goes to set the table.)*

(To **NOAH.***)* Dinner's just about ready.

NOAH. Are you puttin' him to bed?

HARPER. Yeah, it's lights out.

NOAH. I can do it.

HARPER. I got it.

(**HARPER** *goes into Benny's room. Finally alone,* **NOAH** *shivers hard. She spots Harper's sweater and puts it on, sinks her hands in the pockets and pulls out the slip of paper, sees what's on it. She sees the lights go out in Benny's room and takes off the sweater, puts it where it came from.)*

Scene Eight

*(The next morning. **HARPER** is in the middle of a highly efficient pre-work routine: making toast and eggs and coffee, getting dressed, packing her bag and lunch for Benny, all in relative unison. There is a human-sized bundle of blankets on the couch. She calls toward Benny's door:)*

HARPER. We're leaving in five! Five, sweetie, you got that? You open that door now, so you can hear me, alright? It's my first day back in a week and I can't be late, so that's a hard five. One two three four five, and I want a whole minute counted out when you brush your teeth, okay? You're gonna have to eat your eggs in the car. Unless your Aunt Noah steals them from you before you get out here!

(She cranes her neck to peer over toward his room, smiles.)

And, *oh*, and remember to give Mr. Walden the permission slip I signed for your field trip, cause I hear the pre-K field trip might just involve meeting some very interesting animals. *I've* never even been to the Chattaroy Zoo, you lucky boy. You're gonna have to tell me what all those wild animals look like up close.

Ooh, Noah, could you swing by Food City after work, we're nearly out of coffee.

(She gets no response, looks up.)

Hellooo. If you're still sleepin' I'm gonna have to let Benny wake you up, and you know he likes to jump on that couch.

(She puts on her cardigan and fixes her hair while crossing to the couch, sees the bundle of blankets.)

Don't you have work at ten? Noah, I swear –

(She pulls off the blanket to reveal more blankets and pillows, no **NOAH**. *She picks up a pillow and screams into it. She drops the pillow, regains her composure, and runs to her room. She returns, carrying the sweater she was wearing the night before, and turns out the pockets. They're empty. She throws the sweater across the room.)*

Shit. Shit shit shit SHIT.

Nothing Benny I said nothing.

You're gonna eat your eggs in the car, we need to go now. One two three *now.*

(She runs to the door, opens it wide.)

(Screaming out.) NOAH!

Scene Nine

(An hour later. **JACKSON** *has just arrived at the house.)*

HARPER. What took you so –

JACKSON. Came fast as I could.

HARPER. Where were you?

JACKSON. Job interview. Food City. Left soon as I saw you'd / called.

HARPER. Has she called, texted?

JACKSON. Nothing, I wasn't even gonna see her today.

HARPER. Shit.

Job interview?

JACKSON. Food City, yeah. Good not great.

Don't worry, we'll find her.

HARPER. Do you think she's used?

JACKSON. Like I said I haven't –

HARPER. If you had to guess.

JACKSON. I'd guess yeah. If I had to.

HARPER. But nothing *happened,* nothing went *wrong,* she seemed like she was doing so much better –

JACKSON. Nothing has to happen.

HARPER. She didn't take my car, she can't be too far away.

JACKSON. Coulda hitched.

HARPER. Who could've sold it to her, you're supposed to know.

JACKSON. Called every man on that list, on th'way here. Half picked up, said they didn't sell shit.

HARPER. They're drug dealers, they lie.

JACKSON. Hey.

HARPER. It's my fault she got the list, it was in the pocket of the –

If she's high right now it's my fault, or if she's – not safe –

JACKSON. No one's fault, don't work that way. 'Cept the ones getting rich off poor folks dying. Big Pharma, they can burn in / hell.

HARPER. Jackson, you profit off it.

JACKSON. I ain't rich! I try to keep them from dying, I don't get no one new on the habit.

(*A knock on the door.*)

Noah?!

HARPER. Why would Noah knock?

(**AUBREY** *lets herself in.*)

AUBREY. Harper. I got your, all your voicemails. You did the right thing, calling –

HARPER. I don't know what I'm doing.

AUBREY. Breathe, hon. How can I help?

HARPER. Jackson has the addresses. This is Jackson.

JACKSON. Who's she?

AUBREY. This is her dealer?

JACKSON. Whoa.

HARPER. And boyfriend.

JACKSON. Just boyfriend now. She a cop?

AUBREY. No, I'm not.

HARPER. I guess we should start with those addresses.

JACKSON. They're pickup spots, she wouldn't stick around.

HARPER. But nearby.

JACKSON. Maybe nearby. Who's she?

AUBREY. *(Impatient.)* I'm Aubrey.

JACKSON. *(Under* **HARPER** *and* **AUBREY***'s lines.)* But who *are* you, why are you – can anyone tell me anything?

HARPER. How long is it before she's considered missing?

AUBREY. The waiting period's more of a myth. We could report her as missing, but then you'd have authorities to contend with once she's / found.

JACKSON. Nope, no cops.

HARPER. Jackson.

AUBREY. No, he's right.

JACKSON. You sure she's not a cop?

HARPER. Why would she agree with you on that point if she / were a cop?

JACKSON. Cops play tricks.

AUBREY. I'm not a / cop.

JACKSON. Cause you can't lie about it if you are, I know my / rights.

HARPER. The police could help find her, / maybe.

AUBREY. If she's carrying any product, they'll have to detain her.

HARPER. / Shoot.

JACKSON. Bunch of sons-of-bitches.

(*Pause.*)

HARPER. I should've been checking in on her more.

AUBREY. I know how you feel right now, but this is not your fault, hon, I promise you.

HARPER. *(Abruptly.)* I know that. I don't need comforting.

AUBREY. Understood.

JACKSON. How you know Noah?

HARPER. Just ignore him.

JACKSON. Don't ignore me!

AUBREY. I...work with addicts, like your girlfriend.

JACKSON. She can't afford rehab.

HARPER. Can we focus on the task at hand, Jackson.

JACKSON. Ain't like I haven't tried, started saving up money for her to go through one'a those places a couple years back when she was in a real bad way, but I had to give it to Jason for his Iraq leg.

AUBREY. It's not rehab, but we do help addicts.

JACKSON. What kinda help you lookin' to give?

AUBREY. You can ask her when you find her.

JACKSON. I don't like this. Secret meetings and she goes off missing, if you're the reason she's gone I'll –

(**AUBREY** *stands.*)

AUBREY. Sir. Do not threaten me. Don't. Okay?

JACKSON. – I wasn't –

AUBREY. Can I get a verbal affirmation that you understand?

JACKSON. – Okay.

I don't like strangers.

AUBREY. And I do not like drug dealers.

JACKSON. Fine.

AUBREY. Fine. Frankly I think you should be focused on strategies to find your girlfriend at the moment. Because even after a short period of detox, an addict's tolerance wanes significantly.

Her regular dose could now kill her. She's overdosed recently, that increases her risk of overdosing again. The product she's using could very well be cut with Fentanyl.

Her odds do not look so optimal right now, so I'd suggest you redirect your energy toward finding her as soon as possible.

(Beat. **JACKSON** *looks away from* **AUBREY**.*)*

JACKSON. I'll, uh. Head West, toward Cisco Drive.

HARPER. I'll take South Williamson, down to Goody.

AUBREY. Okay. You have a plan, a plan is good.

HARPER. Call me if –

JACKSON. Ditto.

AUBREY. What can I do to help? I know you're not asking, I'm just offering.

HARPER. Ah,

AUBREY. I could take care of Benny, or –

HARPER. Benny. Right. Jesus. I, he's at school, he's –

AUBREY. I'll pick him up.

HARPER. He won't go with a stranger.

AUBREY. Call a neighbor and have them do it, I'll watch him once he's here.

HARPER. Maybe it's a bad / idea.

AUBREY. We'll play, we'll have fun. I'm good with kids.

HARPER. Right.

JACKSON. *(Abruptly.)* What if she's gone?

HARPER. Jesus, Jackson.

JACKSON. She said she'd never leave me, she promised.

HARPER. If she's relapsed, she's probably not thinking about promises.

JACKSON. But –

HARPER. I don't know what to tell you, you're not the only one she made promises to.

We should go.

AUBREY. What should I tell Benny? When he gets home.

HARPER. Benny.

Ah. Tell him something good. Try not to lie.

Scene Ten

*(Late that night. **AUBREY** has fallen asleep at the dinner table. The front door opens, clumsily but slowly. **NOAH** walks in quietly, closing the door behind her. She's trying her best to act sober. She sees **AUBREY**, tiptoes past her toward Benny's room. She pauses – where did she leave it? – goes back to the living room and finds the puzzle under the couch cushions. She picks it up gently, moves toward Benny's room again. **AUBREY** jerks awake. Seeing **NOAH**, she is immediately alert.)*

AUBREY. Oh, gosh, hi.

*(**NOAH** stops in her tracks.)*

NOAH. What are *you* doing here?

AUBREY. I've been watching Benny while –

Noah, does your sister know you're here?

*(**NOAH** snorts.)*

She's been scared out of her mind. So has your boyfriend.

NOAH. I didn't wanna see them. I have a present for Benny.

AUBREY. Are you high? Look at me.

Right, so you're not going to interact with a child that way.

NOAH. I'm just. Going to give him a *puzzle*. I got him a new one.

*(Beat. **NOAH** takes a step toward Benny's room. **AUBREY** counters by moving to block **NOAH**.)*

It's a puzzle of a farm. With cows and pigs.

AUBREY. Okay, I'm sure he'll love it in the morning.

NOAH. I can't give it to'im in the morning.

AUBREY. Why's that?

NOAH. I can't stay here. I broke the rules.

AUBREY. I think your sister cares more that you're safe –

NOAH. I don't *wanna* stay here.

AUBREY. Noah, why would you – what's the appeal of disappearing?

NOAH. I doubt you'd get it.

AUBREY. I, you're right, I don't. I actually really don't but I do get what it does to a family.

How every single time you wait and wait and pray that they'll come back. And then one time they don't, and I get how that feels too.

I mean, aren't you ever scared? That you won't come back?

(Beat.)

NOAH. I'm sorry about your kid.

AUBREY. Thank you.

NOAH. But you're not my mom. So um I don't mean to be rude but this is actually none of your goddamn business.

AUBREY. Professionally, honey, it is my business.

NOAH. Then stop calling me honey. And stop trying to connect with me or whatever and ask about my life like you care, like I'm not just a new walking testimonial for your website or your stupid pamphlet or. Whatever.

(Pause.)

AUBREY. You're right, I was trying to connect with you, but why is that a bad thing?

NOAH. I think what you do is gross.

AUBREY. Okay.

NOAH. No more moms, no more kids, that don't make sense.

AUBREY. It's, as I said it's not a perfect solution / but –

NOAH. It ain't a solution at all, not to this!

AUBREY. There are no solutions to this problem, then, okay? Not really! The only solution is you stop, you get clean and I'm sorry but the odds of that happening are just not good enough to do nothing and watch as you hurt the people around you. As you hurt your son. It's a privilege to be a mother, Noah.

NOAH. That's enough.

AUBREY. And some of us didn't have a say in giving up a child.

NOAH. I said that's enough.

*(Pause. **NOAH** lunges to get past **AUBREY**. **AUBREY** pushes her back.)*

AUBREY. Okay, that's – there's no need for that.

NOAH. Let me see my *goddamn kid*.

AUBREY. How about this, okay, okay? Let me – ask you a few questions. You answer them and – y'know what, you answer them and you can pass. And I'll give up on your case, I'll have done what I can.

NOAH. I don't need to answer your stupid –

AUBREY. Harper said you've been thinking about having children. More children, ones you're involved in raising this time.

NOAH. That the first question? Yup.

AUBREY. No, my question is when?

And how does it fit into your sobriety timeline? By the way – second question – what is that sobriety timeline? How do you intend on getting clean indefinitely? Or would there be any question of you relapsing after kids come around? And in that case – what, would Harper adopt more? Or would Jackson take a long enough break from dealing heroin to take care of them on his own? Incidentally – what happens to the kids when he gets arrested? Or killed, potentially.

And with Jackson still around, or not, what if something goes wrong for you and you want to use? You get in a fight at work, or you see a deal in action on the way to pick up your kid from school. Do you keep driving? Or do you stop? It's so easy to find, isn't it? You have all those numbers now. Even if you never source from Jackson ever again, you know where you could find it. Even if you move to a different town, you know what kind of people to look out for. They know how to look out for you, for that matter.

NOAH. *(Near-inaudible.)* Stop.

AUBREY. Or, forget all those questions, you've had, what, four years to get to know your birth son?

One of those, you were sober, even, right?

Tell me anything meaningful about him. I got to spend a few hours with him tonight, sweet kid, bright kid. Open book. Tell me his first word. What kinds of dreams he has, what he draws in class, who his friends in pre-K are.

(*A long beat.*)

NOAH. He likes puzzles.

AUBREY. Right. What else?

(Long beat.)

*(**NOAH** chews her lip, exhales.)*

NOAH. Christ.

You really believe in what you do, huh?

AUBREY. I believe in doing something to make a difference.
     This isn't pleasant. But it makes a difference, so I do it.

NOAH. Maybe we should. Start over, or.

It's just so hard for me to trust people…

AUBREY. I get it. I totally get it.

NOAH. I believe you.

Maybe I could. Make us a cup of coffee, and.

AUBREY. And I can call your sister,

NOAH. And we can just talk?

AUBREY. Honey, I'd love that.

*(**NOAH** opens her arms for a hug. When
AUBREY moves in, **NOAH** shoves her to the
floor [toward the couch]. Deftly, she kicks
away the doorstop keeping the door open,
and slams it behind her. We see her, through
the glass, bar the door shut. She turns toward
where Benny [unseen] is sleeping and begins
to move toward him.)*

Noah, NOAH. LET ME IN LET ME –

*(**AUBREY** pulls herself up and jiggles the
doorknob.)*

NOAH. *(Offstage.)* Shhh. He's *sleeping.*

Scene Eleven

(Soon after. **HARPER**, **JACKSON** *and* **AUBREY** *are outside the door.* **NOAH** *is still in Harper and Benny's room. We can see* **NOAH** *through the glass, but can't see much further than her pacing form.)*

JACKSON. Noah? Baby, it's me.

NOAH. *(Offstage.)* Hi Jackson.

JACKSON. Can you just come out?

NOAH. *(Offstage.)* I'm not leaving until you promise you won't take him away.

HARPER. Oh this is not the time to make an ultimatum, Noah.

JACKSON. *(Low.)* Baby, you disappeared on me, what was that about?

NOAH. *(Offstage.)* It don't have to do with you.

JACKSON. *You* have to do with me!

NOAH. *(Offstage.) Shh* he's sleeping.

HARPER. This feels a lot like a threat, Noah.

NOAH. *(Offstage.)* Ain't a threat.

HARPER. Just get out of there and we can talk like adults.

NOAH. *(Offstage.)* Are you mad?

HARPER. Of course I'm mad.

NOAH. *(Offstage.)* You're mean when you're mad.

AUBREY. *(Low.)* I still think you should break down the door.

HARPER. *(Low.)* I don't want to frighten Benny.

NOAH. What're y'all sayin'?

HARPER. Come out here and we can say it to you directly.

NOAH. *(Offstage.)* Benny should see me. I'm his, he should see me.

HARPER. We'll talk about it.

NOAH. *(Offstage.)* Stop lying.

HARPER. You're only making things worse, the longer you're in there.

>*(Silence. **NOAH** has retreated past our point of vision. **HARPER** leans in close to the door so she can see clearly through the fogged glass. She gets up and sighs.)*

JACKSON. What's she doing?

HARPER. She's doing a puzzle.

NOAH. *(Offstage.)* He likes to see it made before he does it himself.

HARPER. Noah I swear to – you get *out of there.*

AUBREY. *(A new tactic.)* Nothing has to change if you come out now.

>**(HARPER** *looks at* **AUBREY. AUBREY** *shrugs.)*

NOAH. *(Offstage.)* That's not true.

AUBREY. It is! No one's going to punish you. Mistakes happen, your sister understands.

HARPER. *(Low so only **AUBREY** can hear.)* I do?

AUBREY. *(Low.)* Benny's safety matters most. You just need her out.

NOAH. *(Offstage.)* You're lying.

HARPER. Nope, she's not.

>*(Pause.)*

I won't cut you off from Benny, okay? Just come out.

NOAH. *(Offstage.)* I never got to watch him sleep. I ain't been alone with him since he was born.

HARPER. I know.

NOAH. *(Offstage.)* That makes me sad. It makes me mad.

HARPER. I get it. We can talk about it.

AUBREY. *(Soothing.)* Just unlock the door, hon.

HARPER. Please.

NOAH. *(Offstage.)* You won't take him away?

HARPER. – No.

(Pause. They hold their breaths.)

JACKSON. *Noah they're lyin' to you.*

HARPER. Jackson what the hell is *wrong* with you?!

JACKSON. She deserves to know. I don't want her lied to, that's not love.

AUBREY. Oh my God.

JACKSON. She deserves someone here who wants what's best for her.

HARPER. And that's you? Her *boyfriend* who got her hooked on heroin, you goddamn *imbecile*?

NOAH. *(Offstage.)* You're swearing.

HARPER. You're right, Noah, I'm swearing, I'm gonna break a few of my own rules when my junkie sister is hiding with my son in his goddamn bedroom and I'm having to deal with her / idiotic –

NOAH. *(Offstage.)* You called me a junkie.

(Pause.)

(Offstage.) Do you think I'm a –

HARPER. You gave up after a *week*. How does that look, Noah, look at it from where I'm standing. You want the truth, you want things said straight, then honestly, I'm – disappointed.

NOAH. You hate me?

HARPER. I don't hate you.

I'm sad is all. And scared. Benny's in there.

NOAH. *(Offstage.)* I'm not gonna do anything to'im.

He just looks so peaceful asleep like that.

HARPER. So let him sleep. And unlock the door, and come out here with me. Please?

> (**NOAH** *is silent.*)

JACKSON. You okay, baby?

HARPER. Say something.

Noah?

> *(Pause.)*

NOAH. *(Offstage.)* Um.

Benny's uh he's sort of shakin' / what should –

HARPER. You need to open the door *right now*.

> *(The sound of crying from within.* **HARPER** *tugs at the doorknob relentlessly, starts pounding at the door. The following lines should overlap:)*

NOAH. *(Offstage.)* What's / wrong, Benny?

HARPER. Noah / *let us in.*

AUBREY. *(To* **HARPER**.*)* You / said he gets seizures?

JACKSON. *(Resigned.)* I can / break it open if y'all need me to.

NOAH. *(Offstage.)* He won't let me hold him / why won't –

HARPER. Open the *door, now.*

> (**NOAH** *unlocks the door and* **HARPER** *rushes in past her. Low soothing sounds from* **HARPER** *and the crying subsides.* **AUBREY** *and* **JACKSON** *watch* **HARPER** *mother Benny.* **NOAH** *walks out from the room, looking at no one, and sits on the couch. She buries her face in her hands.)*

Scene Twelve

(Soon after. **AUBREY**, **JACKSON**, **NOAH** *and* **HARPER** *sit around the living room table. Beat.* **HARPER** *speaks flatly and formally, addressing* **NOAH** *but not looking at her:)*

HARPER. Out of courtesy, I'm going to walk you through what's going to happen.

You kidnapped Benny.

JACKSON. You can't kidnap your own kid.

AUBREY. *(Low.)* You can if you don't have custody.

HARPER. You held him hostage, is maybe a more accurate way of putting it and you did it while there was heroin in your system so obviously I have legal precedent to keep you away from him indefinitely, I could get a formal restraining order but I won't do that because. I don't think it's necessary, I think you know you can't see him for a long time, I hope you know that, I hope you're sober enough to grasp that you just bought yourself separation from your birth son until you're one year clean, whenever that is.

JACKSON. She was scared you'd –

HARPER. *(Hard.)* Do not interrupt me or I will send you to jail for trafficking drugs.

(Back to **NOAH**, *flat again.)* I am grateful that you are alive and that you survived this, but I do not trust you anymore. Not just with Benny, at all. You'll be moving out, obviously, I assume back in with Jackson but I do not care, as long as you are not here.

NOAH. *(Soft.)* Harper –

HARPER. Jackson will help you get your things out now.

NOAH. Harper please look at me.

HARPER. I think you owe Aubrey an apology before she leaves, I mean you attacked the woman, you could have seriously hurt her, I think you owe everyone here except probably Jackson an apology but I'm not interested in empty words or promises anymore.

(Beat.)

NOAH. I'm sorry.

AUBREY. I appreciate that.

NOAH. I didn't mean to hurt you. If I did.

AUBREY. I'm fine.

JACKSON. *(Low.)* Honeybee, you don't have to be here if you don't want to.

NOAH. Harper can we talk for a second.

HARPER. I don't think I want to do that, no.

NOAH. Harper look at me please.

JACKSON. I'll get your stuff and bring it out.

NOAH. *(To **JACKSON**.)* Can you wait in the car? I just need a minute.

JACKSON. – Sure, baby.

AUBREY. I'm gonna be on my way, then.

> (**HARPER** *looks down, says nothing.* **JACKSON** *picks up Noah's duffel bag and leaves reluctantly.* **AUBREY** *begins to collect her things.)*

HARPER. You should go too.

NOAH. I can fix this. I just need to think for a –

HARPER. You can think about all this when you are out of my home.

> (**AUBREY** *waits a moment, appraises the situation, and moves to leave as well. Suddenly:)*

NOAH. I'll do it.

Harper I'll do it.

> *(Pause.* **HARPER** *finally looks at* **NOAH**.*)*

HARPER. What?

NOAH. The surgery. The thing.

I'll do it.

> (**NOAH** *and* **HARPER** *look at one another.* **HARPER** *is silent.)*

And the money, it'll all go to Benny. You said he needs help you can't give him, therapy and medicine, tutors to help him learn what doesn't come natural. You decide how to use it but it goes to Benny. I'll do a good thing for him.

AUBREY. I think you're making the responsible choice.

NOAH. I don't know if it's fair but it's right. I think it's right.

(To **AUBREY**.*)* What you said to me. I don't have the right answers. I don't see that far ahead, I don't know what I'd do.

AUBREY. That makes sense, hon.

NOAH. I wanna know. I wanna know I can be good.

AUBREY. I'll take you to the doctor I've been in contact with as soon as his office is open.

> *(Something shifts in* **HARPER**.*)*

HARPER. Wait, just. This is all fast, let's not –

NOAH. This could fix it.

HARPER. What did you say to her?

AUBREY. Nothing that wasn't true.

People like us give and give until we have nothing left.

HARPER. People like us?

AUBREY. Victims of other people's circumstances.

HARPER. Why don't we slow down and talk it through. Just you and me, Noah.

AUBREY. Let her make a good decision. Let her help.

NOAH. I can give Benny a good thing.

(From the other room, groggy, a child's voice:)

BENNY. *(Offstage.)* Mama?

(**NOAH** *and* **HARPER** *both turn, instinctively.* **HARPER** *sees* **NOAH** *turn.)*

End of Play

www.ingramcontent.com/pod-product-compliance
Lightning Source LLC
Chambersburg PA
CBHW070352120726
47909CB00008B/2817